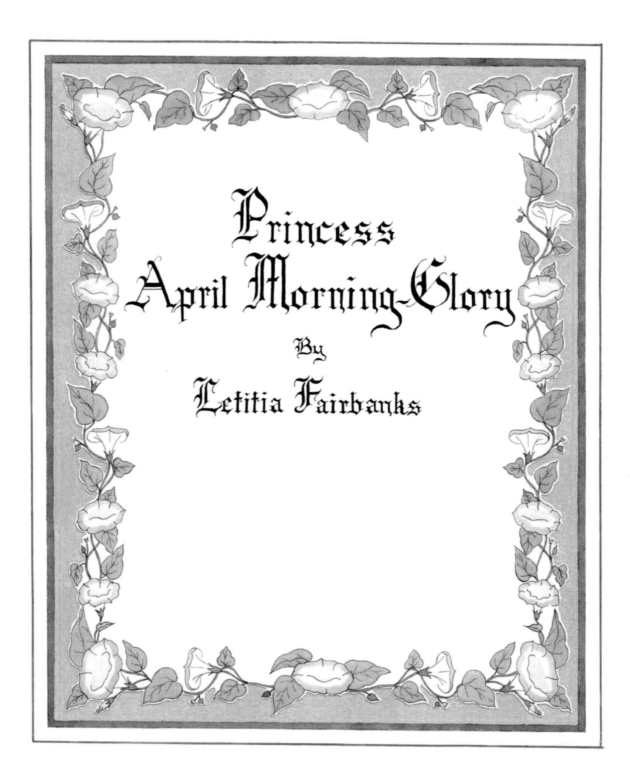

Princess
April Morning-Glory

By

Letitia Fairbanks

Digital restoration by Danny Garrett
DannyGarrett.com

Photograph of Letitia Fairbanks by
Carlyle Blackwell Jr.
for
Paul A. Hesse Studios, 1941
Courtesy of the Blackwell family

For Kelley

Once upon a time the Fairy Queen found a tiny fairy baby in a shiny pink tulip. Tenderly she lifted the fairy baby out of the flower and took her home to the Crystal Castle in the middle of the Enchanted Forest.

The Fairy King was as happy as the Fairy Queen and commanded all his subjects to gather into the Golden Hall to see their child. And as the birds sang a lullabye he touched the fairy baby with his magic wand and named her Princess April Morning-Glory.

And all that night the halls of the castle were filled with laughter as the fairies danced to the gay music of the fairy musicians, ate wild honey and drank sparkling dew in yellow buttercups.

Princess April Morning-Glory was given a plump fairy nurse to watch over her, and like all babies she grew and grew until she became a

little fairy girl with long golden hair and
pretty little dresses which the fairies
wove out of cobwebs. And every
morning after she bathed in a white lily
cup filled with fresh morning dew, the
fairy nurse would comb out her golden
hair with a golden comb.

Then Princess April would ship off to Fairy School to study her lessons. Not reading, writing and arithmetic like other little girls learn, but how to use a magic wand. Because fairies must know how to cast spells, to protect their friends the tiny woodland creatures and most important of all they must know how to grant three wishes.

So Princess April studied all her lessons and was a very good fairy child. But one day her eyes grew sad and she sighed a deep sigh, for her wings were too small to fly and try as hard as she would, she could not soar up into the sky like the grown-up fairies.

This made her so unhappy that everyone in the Crystal Castle began to notice that something was wrong with their little Princess. She no longer smiled and she was cross with her plump fairy nurse. She even spoke sharply to the blue butterfly which the Fairy Queen had given to her for her birthday.

The other fairies shook their heads with fear. Woefully they began

to whisper among themselves that perhaps

Princess April Morning-Glory was be-

coming a wicked fairy and would go to live

in Twilight Forest in the gloomy Jet

Castle of the wicked Fairy Misery.

Then one day when all the good

fairy childen went to school, Princess April decided instead to take a peek at the Great World beyond.

The blue butterfly fluttered faithfully after her and at last they came to the edge of the Enchanted Forest and there just outside the magic boundary sat a big black spider. He smiled craftily and invited her into his web for a cup of honey

"Don't be afraid," he urged. "I will spin you some fine wings."

Princess April hesitated, but the spider's promise of wings was too great a temptation. And in spite of the blue butterfly's warning that if they left the Enchanted Forest they could not return, she stepped over the magic boundary.

"Oh dear, oh dear me," moaned the blue butterfly as he fluttered after her.

Once outside in the Great World, Princess April looked around for the black spider, but he had sneaked away. For he was really a spy for the wicked Fairy Misery and was on his way with the news that Princess April Morning-Glory had left Fairyland.

Immediately Princess April realized that she had been tricked. The Enchanted Forest had vanished and she found herself alone in the Great World with only the blue butterfly to watch over her.

However, she was not afraid for she was a very brave little fairy girl. So she explored the woodland paths and when she was hungry, the friendly bees brought her honey. And when she grew weary a big grasshopper gave her a ride.

"Whee! How wonderful to be out of Fairyland," she said happily.

But that night when it was dark and the wind went Woo-o-o through the unfamiliar trees she changed her mind. For all her gay companions had long since disappeared to their homes and she had no place to go. At last she became so cold and forlorn that she just sat down and cried and cried as if her heart would surely break.

"Whatever will become of us?"
She sobbed to the blue butterfly.

Then she heard a soft, purring
sound and before her stood a large,
white pussy-cat.

"Why are you crying little fairy
girl?" She mewed.

"Because I was naughty and left
Fairyland and now I have no place to
sleep." Princess April replied.

"I can fix that," said the
kind cat. "You can sleep in my ear."

So Princess April Morning-Glory dried her eyes and soon was fast asleep in the pussy-cat's ear with the blue butterfly perched on the tip.

The next morning Princess April took leave of her kind friend and started on her way to find the wise, old owl. For the pussy-cat had told her that he might know the way back to Fairyland.

She searched for the wise, old owl until the sun was high in the sky. And at last when she found him he was sound asleep on the branch of a tall tree.

"Please wake up wise, old owl
and tell me the way back to Fairyland,"
called Princess April.

The owl opened one sleepy eye,
then shook his head for he did not know

the way. But he told her to ask the Wizard who lived in the cave at the edge of the forest.

"He knows everything," hooted the owl wisely.

There was nothing to do but to follow his advice, so Princess April hurried on and the blue butterfly had to fly very fast to keep up with her.

Just as the sun was setting they reached the edge of the forest and found the Wizard's cave. And there sat the Wizard in a dark, flowing robe

sprinkled with silver stars.

"Hello," said Princess April timidly.

"You're Princess April Morning-Glory," he replied as he looked up from the ponderous book he was reading.

"How did you know?" she asked in amazement.

"I know everything," he replied solemnly.

Then he opened another large book to page 501.

"To return to Fairyland," he read,

"One must first do three good deeds."

Then the Wizard warned Princess April to beware of the wicked Fairy Misery who even now searched for her amid the shadowed forest and lonely fields.

"Return to me when your third good deed has been done," commanded the Wizard, "then I will tell you how to reach the crest of the rainbow down which you can slide back into Fairyland."

The next morning Princess April and the blue butterfly set forth and they

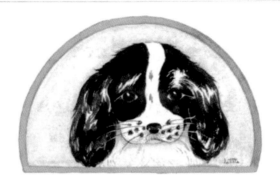

had not gone far when they found a tiny,
black and white puppy who had lost it's
mother.

"Come with us," said Princess
April, "We will find you a good home."
So the three of them walked on
until they came to a charming pink and
white house. Cautiously, they entered
the yard and peeked in the window.
And there in bed, lay a little

boy who was sick. Tears glistened in his brown eyes for he was very sad.

"Hello," said Princess April. "Why are you crying?"

"Because I'm lonely and have no one to play with."

So Princess April sat on the window sill and told him all about herself and the puppy without a home.

"If he will stay with me I will be very good to him," replied the little boy.

So the puppy leaped up on his bed

and licked his face and wagged his tail and the little boy laughed because he was happy and now had a playmate.

Later when the little boy fell asleep with the puppy in his arms, Princess April quietly departed. And late that afternoon she found a beautiful bird lying on the ground for his wing had been broken.

Fortunately, she knew just what to do as she had learned how to mend broken wings in Fairy School. First, she took a straight twig and bound it

to the wing with her hair ribbon. Then
she covered it with clay to form a cast.
For many days she and the blue
butterfly carefully nursed the beautiful bird back to health.   At night
they covered him with leaves to keep

him warm and fed him certain healing herbs that Princess April gathered from the fields.

At last when his wing was as good as new, the beautiful bird told Princess April to climb upon his back and he would fly her to the distant castle beyond the hill.

"I go to sing to the Princess who is kept locked in the tower," said the beautiful bird as he soared high in the sky with Princess April and the blue butterfly holding fast to his feathers.

At last they came to rest on the
balcony of the high tower and the beautiful bird sang a lilting song to the
lonely Princess who was as kind as she
was beautiful.

And she was so delighted with

the song and so enchanted with Princess April and the blue butterfly that it was the first happy day she had known since being locked in the tower.

Her wicked uncle, the King, had imprisoned her because she would not marry King Thunderdum who was ugly and cruel but rich and powerful. Instead, she loved Prince Chivalry who lived in the small kingdom west of the Purple Lake.

"Though I languish in this tower till I die," sighed the Princess, "I shall marry no one but my true love."

"Perhaps the Prince will rescue you," said Princess April.

"Impossible," replied the Princess, "This tower is guarded day and night and the King has the only key which hangs always at his side."

To this Princess April Morning-
Glory said nothing, but she had formed
a plan. So once more she mounted the
beautiful bird and they flew to the
Castle of Prince Chivalry. After she
told him her plan, the Prince ordered
out his fastest, white horse and prom-
ised to be at the tower that very night.

When Princess April returned she found the Princess in tears, for the King had told her that King Thunderdum would arrive at sundown and on the morrow she would become his bride.

"Weep not, sweet Princess," said Princess April. "All hope is not yet lost."

Late that night when the Sandman arrived, Princess April begged for a sack of his sleep giving sand. Then she crept into the feasting hall where the two Kings and their followers were

gathered in celebration. She was so

tiny that no one saw her enter and pour

the sand of sleep into the jugs of wine.

As soon as everyone was fast as-

leep from the effects of the drugged wine,

Princess April took the key to the tower

from the wicked King's belt and hastened to meet Prince Chivalry.

It was no time at all until he had disarmed the guards with the aid of his flashing sword. And before more help could arrive, Prince Chivalry unlocked the iron door and carried the Princess down the winding stairs to his waiting, white horse.

They rode all that night at a fast pace for the soldiers of the King were in hot pursuit. But at break of day they reached the Prince's Kingdom

west of the Purple Lake and were safe
at last!

The days that followed were joy-
ous ones. The Princess was married to
her true love, Prince Chivalry and they
gave Princess April a lovely new dress
with a long train for the wedding.

And so great was their gratitude
that the Prince wished to build a tiny,
golden castle for Princess April so that
she could live with them always. But
as Princess April longed to return to
Fairyland, she bade them farewell and

promising to return one day, started on her way to the Wizards' cave.

But she had not gone far when a vulture swooped down from the sky and clasping Princess April in one talon and the blue butterfly in the other, flew off to the gloomy Jet Castle of the wicked Fairy Misery in Twilight Forest.

Although Princess April was very frightened, she bit her lip to keep from crying as she was too proud to let the wicked Fairy Misery see her tears. Nor would she utter a single word.

This made the wicked Fairy so angry that she cast Princess April into a dark dungeon. And every day she came to tempt her with the choicest jewels, silken dresses and bright colored wings.

If Princess April would serve her and do evil instead of good, these priceless gifts would be hers.

But Princess April would not even look at the gifts. So at last the Fairy Misery lost all patience and had her taken to the Magic room where she was preparing a spell to cast over the poor little Princess.

"Once this blue mist has enveloped you," hissed the wicked Fairy, "You will become a little black imp and be my willing servant in all things evil."

Now Princess April really did begin to cry. And the blue butterfly tried to comfort her by saying:

"Weep not, sweet Princess, all hope is not yet lost."

"No, but almost," sobbed Princess April.

Just then, a humming-bird flying near the Jet Castle, saw Princess April and the blue butterfly in the window. Almost as quickly as a flash of lightning he flew to Fairyland and told the Fairy King what he had seen.

The Fairy King realized there was no time to be lost and as the humming-bird could fly faster than anyone else in Fairyland, he gave him his magic wand to carry to Princess April Morning-Glory.

The humming-bird arrived just as the blue mist was about to envelop her and gave her the magic wand. Princess April waved it about her and the blue mist disappeared at once. Then she snatched the wicked fairy's Wishing Ring from its magic pedestal and hopped upon the humming-bird's back with the blue butterfly

holding fast to her shoulder.

The humming-bird flew out the window and high up into the sky. He flew very fast because the wicked Fairy Misery was close upon them in her air chariot drawn by six black bumble bees.

Just as the Wicked Fairy was about to fling a large net about them, the humming-bird reached the crest of the rainbow and they slid safely down into the enchanted realm of Fairyland.

All that day there was great rejoicing in the Crystal Castle because of the return of their dear Princess. And the fairies decided to award her with her wings on the following day.

For although Princess April had been naughty in leaving Fairyland, she had done three good deeds. She had resisted the temptations of the wicked Fairy Misery. And most important of all, she had captured the wicked Fairy's Wishing Ring. As it would take the Fairy Misery fifty years to make another one, during this time Mankind

would dwell in happiness.

That night when Princess April was tucked in her own little bed, the Fairy King touched her forehead with his magic wand and she fell into a deep sleep.

The next day when the Fairy Queen awakened her, a miracle had happened! For Princess April Morning-Glory had grown up during the night!

The fairies dressed her in a gown of dazzling beauty fashioned from star dust. Then in the Golden Hall amid a splendorous ceremony, the Fairy King awarded her with gossamer wings. They were the most beautiful ones in all of Fairy-land as the fairies had woven them from the colors of the rainbow and sprinkled the edges with sunbeams!

And to this day Princess April has been doing good deeds throughout the World. And if you wish very hard for something good, you can be very sure that your wish will be granted by none other than sweet Princess April Morning-Glory!

The End

Photograph of Letitia Fairbanks by Carlyle Blackwell Jr. for Paul A. Hesse Studios

AFTERWORD

Princess April Morning-Glory, a children's book written and illustrated in 1941 by Letitia Fairbanks, the niece of Douglas Fairbanks Sr. and Mary Pickford, emerges as a long-lost treasure from the golden age of Hollywood.

Viewed as unconventional when it first debuted, since the female protagonist chose a career in wish-making over a life of domestic bliss, the story paid homage to and referenced then-current cultural touchstones in a prescient acknowledgment that we create our destinies by the choices that we make.

Like Princess April, Letitia Fairbanks was a woman before her time. Born in 1913, Letitia, the daughter of Robert and Lorie Fairbanks, spent the first six years of her life in Provo, Utah. It was there that her father, an electrical engineer, busied himself designing and building the hydroelectric dams necessary to power the West.

Meanwhile, Robert's younger brother Douglas Fairbanks, who was already a Broadway actor in New York City, set his sights on Hollywood and the brand-new world of motion pictures. In 1919, Douglas joined forces with Mary Pickford, Charlie Chaplin, and D.W. Griffith to form United Artists. Robert Fairbanks, with his engineering and construction background, was appointed as production manager of the new film studio.

The young family relocated to Hollywood, where Letitia and her younger sister, Lucile, came of age alongside the creative energy of her talented uncle and spirited aunt. Pickfair, Douglas and Mary's lavish Beverly Hills estate, was a frequent and much beloved meeting spot.

Early in life, Letitia forged an identity as an artist, specifically as a painter and a writer, leaving theater and film to other members of her family. As a young twenty-something, she began work on Princess April Morning-Glory. Letitia used a calligrapher's pen to write and watercolors to illustrate, interspersed with liberal doses of gold and silver leaf.

While the first copyright of *Princess April Morning-Glory* was granted in 1941, it included only the text of the story, published as a simple pamphlet. The printing technology of the day made reproduction of the original water-color artwork on handmade, oversized paper prohibitively expensive – even for a Fairbanks.

Letitia used an ensemble of current celluloid legends as inspirations for her illustrations. Movie stars like John Barrymore, whose stern countenance embodied the Wicked King, and her cousin Douglas Fairbanks Jr., whose natural demeanor made for an easy Prince Chivalry, were rendered in vivid brush strokes after passing through the lens of Letitia's equally-vivid imagination.

Similar to her protagonist, Letitia felt determined to forge a life on her own terms, independent from her famous, and at times overbearing, family. One of the sources of longtime disagreement between mother and daughter was Letitia's refusal to marry among the allotment of Hollywood's eligible bachelors. Letitia found refuge in Princess April, who came to feel at home in the world not by seeking companionship outside of herself but within herself – ultimately coming to the realization that we are only ever able to grant our own wishes by overcoming our own obstacles.

Holding firm to her artistic identity, Letitia gravitated toward portraiture, landscapes, and still lifes. She was also a biographer, co-authoring *Douglas Fairbanks: The Fourth Musketeer*, with Ralph Hancock. Her marriage to Hal Smoot in 1966 marked the beginning of a particularly joyful and creative period. Needlepoints and annual Christmas cards, which featured a painting from the previous year, not to mention her role as a wife, mother, stepmother and grandmother, brought her much fulfillment.

And after a life rich in artistic accomplishment, Letitia passed away in September of 1992. But Princess April still lives on.

Amanda Letitia Millner-Fairbanks
New York City
July 2012

Amanda Letitia Millner-Fairbanks is the granddaughter of Letitia Fairbanks. She is a graduate of Smith College and Columbia University's Graduate School of Journalism. As a journalist, her work has appeared in The New York Times, the Boston Globe, Newsweek, and The Huffington Post, among other publications.

ACKNOWLEDGEMENTS

Many people were instrumental in bringing *Princess April Morning-Glory* to print, and here are a few that I would personally like to thank:

To my mother, Sue Ashby Smoot, I give thanks for giving me the most enlightened childhood– rearing me in New York City with exposure to soak in all manner of teachings, culture, and life. Without my mother and the brave choices she made – choices which were against the norms of society at that time and the wishes of her father and my father – none of the rest of this story would have unfolded, or at least not in this particular fashion.

A hearty thank-you to the late Louise Carter Green for being the first and persistent voice to urge me to find a publisher, and the continued encouragement to "keep looking." To Betty Jackson, my very own Auntie Mame, I owe a couple of lifetimes of advice, love, and comfort. To the Farr family of Salt Lake City, the love & care you showed Letitia and my Dad in the last years of their lives is greatly appreciated – thank you ever so much.

To Lorain Day, Bronwyn Dutton, and the late Dianne Haworth, all of New Zealand – thank you for recognizing the gem in *Princess April Morning-Glory* and keeping the project moving towards its appropriate spiritual home.

A very special thank-you to Vera Fairbanks for her approval of the participation of her husband, Douglas Fairbanks, Jr., Letitia's inspiration for Prince Chivalry. It was perfect casting, as the word "chivalry" is the best description for the most gracious, charming man that was Letitia's beloved cousin Doug.

To Robert, Bryan, and Amanda thank you for accepting me into your family and including me in your lives.

To my loving, gracious, accepting, and talented husband Danny Garrett – you're second only to Letitia in being the reason we can now enjoy print and digital copies of *Princess April Morning-Glory*. For this and so much more, I love you.

To my father, Harold Nibley Smoot, thank you for your love, your care and attention, your excellent taste, fine style, and offering loving encouragement, even while I pursued a career that you would not have chosen for me. But that's my Dad – always encouraging and urging me and Letitia onward, down the path we desired for ourselves. And thanks for the tips & hints on the care & feeding of an Artist – your training has been put to good use.

My earliest memory of Letitia is during our first visit in the summer of 1967, just before Dad married Tish, as only close family called her. I stayed in her house in North Hollywood, where she had turned her art studio into a little girl's bedroom: one wall covered in blue cloth, with a half-circle bed pushed up against it, with a bed cover made of the same blue cloth. Along the edge of the bed, then extending up onto the wall, was a filigree of white lace, stitched & positioned so that the bed appeared to be enclosed in the petals of a flower that was opening. "Who is this for?" I asked, because I couldn't conceive of anyone creating such an elaborate bedroom for me. That was my introduction to the Fairbanks style – first class, inventive, elegant, creative, and always beautiful!

While my Dad was alive I didn't get to know Letitia as well as I did afterward, when we both held tight to one another – each being the others' common link to Dad. We talked a lot those last four years of Letitia's life. She told me stories that I hadn't heard before, and we went through family photo albums and reminisced. As a lifelong artist who painted up until a month before her death, her every motion was creative.

With her deep spirituality and refusal to reduce the magical to the mundane, Letitia was a unique influence in my life. Through *Princess April Morning-Glory* I hope everyone can have a taste of this fabulous Fairbanks that I was fortunate enough to walk with, for at least a part of my life.

Please remember to do three good deeds, every day. "It's an elegant habit, that once cultivated, will assist all who engage it fully." It will also spread joy, love, and life – the very qualities Letitia possessed and would want her artwork to promote and multiply in the world.

Kelley Smoot Garrett
San Marcos, Texas
December 2012

Kelley Smoot Garrett is the step-daughter of Letitia Fairbanks and the daughter of Harold and Sue Smoot. She's undertaken many projects in her life, but publishing Letitia's masterpiece has been the most fun of all! She lives outside of Austin, Texas, with her husband Danny, along with Louie & Cleo, two cats from New Zealand, a wise old American barn kitty, and a happy only-dog, Moxie.

10 Suggestions for Doing 3 Good Deeds

1. A good deed is something you do to help someone else, not yourself.

"You can sleep in my ear."

2. A good deed is a simple action, thought, or emotion (the energy you give off) that makes the day happier and more joyful than it would have been for another person, living creature or the planet.

Share some laughter with a friend.

Quote from Douglas Fairbanks' 1917 book "Laugh and Live"
Laughter clings to good health as naturally as the needle clings to the magnet. It is the outward expression of an unburdened soul. It bubbles forth as a fountain, always refreshing, always wholesome and sweet.
Douglas Fairbanks, Laugh and Live (Kindle Locations 136-137). Kindle edition.

3. A good deed is done spontaneously. You can't prepare to do a good deed; it's an opportunity that presents itself during the course of your day, as you go about your life, and that you have the choice to accept or decline.

"And late that afternoon she found a beautiful bird lying on the ground for his wing had been broken."

4. A good deed is always done with the heartfelt intention of helping another person, living creature or the planet and cannot contain a lie.

Contrast:

"I go to sing to the Princess who is kept locked in the tower,"

With:

"He smiled craftily and invited her into his web for a cup of honey. "Don't be afraid," he urged. "I will spin you some fine wings."

5. A good deed cannot be measured by money, but instead by something much more precious: the loving intent you hold in your heart when you perform it.

"And every day [Fairy Misery] came to tempt [Princess April] with the choicest jewels, silken dresses and bright colored wings. If Princess April would serve her and do evil instead of good, these priceless gifts would be hers. But Princess April would not even look at the gifts."

Quote from Douglas Fairbanks' 1918 "Making Life Worth While"
There are things that money won't buy, for instance, a good night's sleep.... So we come quickly back to the proposition that wealth, while useful to the stomach and the back, has no purchasing power with the soul. Happiness is a soul quality...
Douglas Fairbanks, Making Life Worth While (Kindle Locations 562-564; 551-553). Kindle edition.

Continued (over)

6. A good deed is committed without consideration of what the Do-er will receive in return.

"And so great was their gratitude that the Prince wished to build a tiny, golden castle for Princess April so that she could live with them always."

Quote from Douglas Fairbanks' 1917 book "Laugh and Live"
And let us not plume ourselves because of our virtue. Personal honesty is our due to ourselves and our fellow man.
Douglas Fairbanks, Laugh and Live (Kindle Locations 424-426). Kindle edition.

> And so great was their gratitude that the Prince wished to build a tiny, golden castle for Princess April so that she could live with them always.

7. The Do-er of a good deed is always rewarded. But some time may pass between the good deed and the reward, which, like the good deed, is not measured by money or material possessions.

> For although Princess April had been naughty in leaving Fairyland, she had done three good deeds.

"A good deed is never lost; he who sows courtesy reaps friendship, and he who plants kindness gathers love."
- St. Basil

"For although Princess April had been naughty in leaving Fairyland, she had done three good deeds."

8. Doing a good deed is like a mirror. It's a reflection of where you can help another, in a manner that will help you, too.

"Fortunately, she knew just what to do as she had learned how to mend broken wings in Fairy School."

> Fortunately, she knew just what to do as she had learned how to mend broken wings in Fairy School.

9. A good deed never involves doing harm to any other, even if the result could be considered good. In other words, if a person invokes "the ends justify the means," that is not a good deed. A good deed is always done wisely and with kindness.

> As soon as everyone was fast asleep from the effects of the drugged wine, Princess April took the key to the tower from the wicked Kings belt and hastened to meet Prince Chivalry.

"As soon as everyone was fast asleep from the effects of the drugged wine, Princess April took the key to the tower from the wicked King's belt and hastened to meet Prince Chivalry."

Note on #9: Princess April doesn't kill anyone. She merely temporarily incapacitates them, leaving them to live and lick their wounds; note there is no revenge on the part of the vanquished. This is a far cry from the modern example, endlessly repeated, of lethal violence as the only solution to all problems that surround us – and our children. Let us return to non-violent solutions to life's problems.

10. A good deed doesn't have to be witnessed to be effective. You may be the only person who knows your good deed was done, and that's perfect.

"First, she took a straight twig and bound it to the wing with her hair ribbon. Then she covered it with clay to form a cast."

Remember:

*What kind of world would you create
if you had to do three good deeds
to make it home again?*

That's your choice. Have fun answering *that* question in your own unique way!

First, she took a straight twig and bound it to the wing with her hair ribbon. Then she covered it with clay to form a cast.

To learn more about Princess April's *Do Three Good Deeds* initiative, visit
Do3GoodDeeds.com and PrincessApril.com

Made in the USA
Middletown, DE
09 March 2022

62338907R00038